TABLE OF CONTENTS

IMAGES

Christmas

Concept and text:
Émilie Beaumont

Illustrations:
Colette David
Yvette Barbetti

Translation:
Lara M. Andahazy

FLEURUS

CHRISTMAS TRADITIONS

BEFORE THERE WAS CHRISTMAS

Christmas, the great Christian holiday, replaced other celebrations that used to take place at the same time every year all across Europe.

In Rome, everything was topsy-turvy from December 17 to 24—slaves ordered around their masters who had to serve them dinner.

Houses were cleaned and decorated with holly and pine trees.

The king of the celebration was chosen from among the young soldiers.

The god Mithra was also worshiped. You can see him wrestling with a bull to the left. On December 25, bulls were sacrificed and their blood poured on the fields to make the earth more fertile and improve harvests.

In Rome, on the same day—the day with the longest night—people celebrated the return of the sun represented by a new-born baby.

At Christmas time in Sweden, Norway and Denmark, people still place a straw goat in front of their houses or near the Christmas tree. This custom comes from the days when the people worshiped Thor, the god of thunder, who is shown on the left in his chariot pulled by goats.

CHRISTMAS—THE BIRTH OF JESUS

Christians chose December 25 to celebrate the birth of Jesus even though the Bible does not give the exact date. Christmas is the birthday of the Son of God.

Mary lived in Nazareth, in Israel. She was going to get married soon.

Her future husband's name was Joseph. He was a carpenter.

One day, the angel Gabriel, God's messenger, visited Mary.

He said, "You have been chosen to be the mother of God's son, Jesus."

MARY'S SECRET

Mary wanted to share her secret and her joy. She went to see her cousin Elizabeth who would be able to give her good advice.

Mary finally arrived. Elizabeth was old and expecting her first child. She said to Mary, "The angel Gabriel visited me too. He told me that my son would prepare the hearts of the people for the coming of Jesus. He will be called John the Baptist."

Joseph loved Mary but when he learned that she was pregnant he refused to marry her. An angel of God appeared to him and said, "Don't be afraid to marry Mary. Her child has no human father for he is the son of God." Reassured, Joseph married Mary.

TO BETHLEHEM

When Jesus was about to be born Joseph and Mary had to go to Bethlehem where Joseph's ancestors had lived.

Everyone had to go to their home towns to be counted for the census.

Mary packed provisions and the clothes that she had prepared for the baby.

Mary traveled on the back of a donkey but the road was long, very long. They were ᵊr so glad to see the outskirts of town!

THE BIRTH OF JESUS

Mary and Joseph were exhausted. Mary knew her baby would soon be born. Would they be able to find an inn for the night?

They went all over town but no one had room for them.

Luckily, a kind innkeeper let them stay in his stable for the night.

And that is where the baby Jesus was born. Mary wrapped him in swaddling clothes.

She laid him in a manger full of straw.

13

GOOD NEWS

In the nearby fields, shepherds were watching over their flocks. Suddenly, in the middle of the night, a bright light filled the sky!

The amazed shepherds were worried. What was happening? Then angels appeared and said, "Do not be afraid, we bring glad tidings!"

Angels announced the birth of Jesus, the Savior of the world sent by God. The shepherds immediately set out in search of the long-awaited child.

THE SHEPHERDS' ADORATION

The shepherds showed their joy in front of Jesus in the manger and repeated the angels' message to Mary and Joseph.

MIDNIGHT MASS

Jesus' birth is celebrated in churches during Midnight Mass.

In cold countries, some people ride sleds to mass.

In the past, people walked to church carrying lanterns to light their way.

In some churches the priest would tell the story of Jesus' birth and then shepherds would arrive and offer him a lamb before bowing to the altar.

JOY TO THE WORLD

Joy to the world! the Lord is come;
Let earth receive her King;
Let every heart prepare him room,
and heaven and nature sing,
and heaven and nature sing,
and heaven, and heaven and nature sing.

Joy to the earth! the Savior reigns;
Let men their songs employ;
while fields and floods,
rocks, hills and plains
Repeat the sounding joy,
Repeat the sounding joy,
Repeat, repeat the sounding joy.

No more let sins and sorrow grow,
nor thorns infest the ground;
He comes to make his blessings flow
far as the curse is found,
far as the curse is found,
far as, far as the curse is found.

He rules the world with truth and grace,
and makes the nations prove
the glories of his righteousness,
and wonders of his love,
and wonders of his love,
and wonders, wonders of his love.

O CHRISTMAS TREE

O Christmas tree, O Christmas tree,
How are thy leaves so verdant!
O Christmas tree, O Christmas tree,
How are thy leaves so verdant!

Not only in the summertime,
But even in winter is thy prime.
O Christmas tree, O Christmas tree,
How are thy leaves so verdant!

O Christmas tree, O Christmas tree,
Much pleasure doth thou bring me!
O Christmas tree, O Christmas tree,
Much pleasure doth thou bring me!

For every year the Christmas tree,
Brings to us all both joy and glee.
O Christmas tree, O Christmas tree,
Much pleasure doth thou bring me!

SILENT NIGHT

Silent night, holy night,
All is calm, all is bright
Round yon virgin mother and child!
Holy infant so tender and mild,
Sleep in heavenly peace.
Sleep in heavenly peace.

Silent night, holy night
Shepherds quake at the sight,
Glories stream from heaven afar,
Heavenly hosts sing alleluia;
Christ the Savior, is born!
Christ the Savior, is born!

Silent night, holy night,
Son of God, love's pure light
Radiant beams from thy holy face,
With the dawn of redeeming grace,
Jesus, Lord, at thy birth.
Jesus, Lord, at thy birth.

ANGELS WE HAVE HEARD ON HIGH

Angels we have heard on high,
Singing sweetly through the night,
And the mountains in reply
Echoing their brave delight.
Gloria in excelsis Deo!
Gloria in excelsis Deo!

Come to Bethlehem and see
Him whose birth the angels sing;
Come, adore on bended knee
Christ, the Lord, the new-born King.
Gloria in excelsis Deo!
Gloria in excelsis Deo!

CHRISTMAS EVE

In the past, the whole family—parents, grandparents, and children—gathered around the fireplace on Christmas Eve.

Children would sing Christmas carols and listen to stories told by their grandparents while a yule log burned in the fireplace.

THE YULE LOG

In the old days a huge tree trunk was burnt in the fireplace. These days in France the yule log has been replaced by a special cake.

Hard wood was chosen for the yule log so that it would burn a long time.

The yule log was decorated with leaves and ribbons before being carried home.

The yule log was laid in the fireplace and lit by the oldest and youngest children after being blessed by the head of the family with oil or spirits.

SAINT FRANCIS OF ASSISI'S CRECHE

At Christmas time a manger scene is set up in every church and every home that celebrates the birth of Jesus.

This ancient custom is said to have been created by Saint Francis of Assisi. One Christmas night Saint Francis organized a play about the birth of Jesus using animals and actors from Grecchio, a small Italian town near Assisi. A baby played the part of Jesus and was laid in a straw-filled manger between a mule and a bull. Everyone carried torches and candles to light up the night. This tradition was taken up by other monks and spread to all the churches. Over time, the actors were replaced by wax or clay figurines.

THE CRECHE TRADITION

In many countries people set up creches in their homes at Christmas time in order to remind themselves that this holiday celebrates the coming of baby Jesus.

France holds the world record for the largest creche. It covered over one and a half square miles (ask a grown-up how big that is). At Christmas time, in Paris, a huge tent is set up in the square in front of city hall to hold a creche from a different country each year. The pictures on this page show parts of a Sicilian creche that was set up in the French capital.

CHRISTMAS SANTONS

In France, the clay figurines of the baby Jesus, Joseph, Mary, the shepherds and so on that are used in creches are called "Santons" which means "little saints."

After the mold is made it is filled with a lump of clay.

The two halves of the mold are squeezed together very tightly. The santon is taken out and let dry for a few days before it is fired in a kiln.

The santons are then decorated with oil-based paint. They are painted in bright, pretty colors.

CHRISTMAS GREENERY

Everyone in the family is helping put up the Christmas decorations. Red and green are traditional Christmas colors.

| holly | mistletoe | ivy | rosemary |

Decorating the house with greenery is a very ancient custom. Even before Christmas existed, people decorated their houses to celebrate the end of the long winter nights. Holly's prickly leaves represent Christ's crown of thorns and its red berries represent drops of his blood. Mistletoe is said to bring good luck. Rosemary symbolizes friendship and ivy, affection.

STRAW—A CRECHE SYMBOL

Many Swedish customs have involved the use of straw for a very long time—well before people started to celebrate Christmas.

Straw was spread on the floor to chase away evil spirits.

Beds were prepared for the dead in case they came back to earth.

The whole family slept on the floor. This custom has continued as part of Christmas traditions because they think people shouldn't sleep more comfortably than Jesus did.

WHERE CHRISTMAS TREES COME FROM

The first descriptions of Christmas trees come from the Alsace region in France. They were set up in the town square.

Pageants took place in front of churches on Christmas Eve. People danced around the tree of Eden symbolized by a pine tree decorated with apples.

CHRISTMAS TREES IN ALSACE

The Christmas tree tradition was carried rapidly out of Alsace by merchants who traveled from town to town.

People cut their Christmas trees in the forest under the watchful eyes of a guard.

At first, the tree was hung from the ceiling with an apple attached to its trunk.

Later, people started to put their Christmas trees in tubs full of sand.

Parents would shake the trees to make small cookies and toys fall out of them.

BUYING YOUR CHRISTMAS TREE

People buy their Christmas trees either on Christmas Eve or several days earlier, depending on the traditions of the country they live in. They are generally taken down on January 6.

The whole family can help choose the Christmas tree. What fun!

You can buy Christmas trees with or without their roots.

Some Christmas trees lose their needles, others do not.

If you buy one with its roots, you can plant it in your garden after Christmas

DECORATING THE TREE

At first, Christmas trees were decorated with fruits—mostly apples—and later people added candy, cookies, garlands and balls.

In the old days, people decorated their trees with twelve candles. They represented the twelve months of the year. People also sprinkled flour on their trees to imitate snow.

In some countries Christmas trees are decorated with garlands of flags. In others, people use beautiful colored bows.

SETTING THE TABLE

In the old days, people would put three different-sized white tablecloths on the table for Christmas dinner. The table should be a festive sight.

CHRISTMAS EVE DINNER

In many countries, people traditionally eat their Christmas Eve dinner in the middle of the night, either before or after Midnight Mass.

The traditional Christmas Eve dinner in France is made up of oysters, foie gras, smoked salmon, white sausage, stuffed turkey and a special cake called a "bûche" (yule log). Some families eat left over turkey for Christmas lunch.

In Poland, twelve different dishes are served on Christmas Eve. The dishes vary from family to family. A few examples are: cep mushroom or beet soup, cabbage ravioli, poppy seed pasta and much more.

An American Christmas Eve dinner: corn, stuffed turkey, pumpkin pie and vanilla ice cream.

A Spanish Christmas Eve dinner: almond soup, roast fish, roast goose (in some families) and *turrón* (a kind of nougat).

A Hungarian Christmas Eve dinner: fish soup, breaded fish, French fries and a cake roll called *beigli*.

In Italy, Christmas Eve dinner varies from region to region: eel, turkey and chestnuts, cake (either *panettone* or *zelten*).

A Swedish Christmas Eve dinner: marinated herring, meat balls, roast ham and cabbage, rice pudding and small ginger cookies.

An English Christmas Eve dinner: roast ham, roast turkey stuffed with Brussels sprouts or peas, baked potatoes and Christmas pudding (a kind of fruit cake).

A Portuguese Christmas Eve dinner: different kinds of cooked cod with cabbage and potatoes, a roast turkey stuffed with chestnuts and French toast for dessert.

A German Christmas Eve dinner: herring salad, roast goose with red and green cabbage, apples and prunes, and lots of desserts—spice cakes, honey cakes, gingerbread, etc.

OPEN-AIR CHRISTMAS MARKETS

Many cities have open-air Christmas markets. You can find everything you need to decorate your house and tree.

Open-air Christmas markets are lots of fun. They sell delicious candies and cakes.

A Santa Clause marching band announces the opening of the market.

A huge music box plays jolly Christmas carols.

Visiting the market can give you a healthy appetite. Father is eating a grilled sausage and the children are eating Christmas cookies.

GREETING CARDS

Christmas greeting cards were invented in England. The very first card showed a family and children wishing each other a merry Christmas. 1000 of these cards were sold.

You can find any kind of greeting card you want in the United States. In other countries there are a lot less cards to chose from. You can also make your own cards to send to people you care about.

In England, like in America, many people decorate their living rooms with the greeting cards they get at Christmas time.

SAINT NICHOLAS

In Belgium and certain parts of Germany, Switzerland, Austria, France and Holland, Saint Nicholas brings Christmas gifts to children on December 6.

Nicholas was a very generous bishop. He is known for his many miracles that helped children. The picture below shows his most famous miracle—bringing three children back to life after an innkeeper killed them and hid them in a barrel.

Do you know the tune to "Jolly Old Saint Nick"?

JOLLY OLD SAINT NICK

Jolly old Saint Nicholas
Lean your ear this way!
Don't you tell a single soul
What I'm going to say;
Christmas Eve is coming soon;
Now, you dear old man,
Whisper what you'll bring to me;
Tell me if you can.

When the clock is striking twelve,
When I'm fast asleep,
Down the chimney broad and black,
With your pack you'll creep;
All the stockings you will find
Hanging in a row;
Mine will be the shortest one,
You'll be sure to know.

Johnny wants a pair of skates;
Susie wants a dolly;
Nellie wants a story book;
She thinks dolls are folly;
As for me, my little brain
Isn't very bright;
Choose for me, old Santa Claus,
What you think is right.

LEGENDS ABOUT SAINT NICHOLAS

Another legend tells of Saint Nicholas's kind gifts to poor, hungry children who lived in a large city by the sea.

Saint Nicholas gathered fruits, vegetables and grains of wheat. He loaded it all onto a large ship with blue sails and set out for the city.

Saint Nicholas knocked on the children's doors and left bags of wheat, fruit and vegetables on the doorsteps. The happy children rushed to the food. Ever since, he comes back down to earth every year to bring presents to children.

SAINT NICHOLAS IN HOLLAND

In Holland, children are told that Saint Nicholas lives in Spain with his faithful servant, Black Peter. They arrive on December 6 on a big ship.

All year long Saint Nicholas writes down children's good and bad deeds while his servant works hard to prepare the presents.

Saint Nicholas and Black Peter are met by the mayor and the queen. The servant's head is covered with soot because he's the one who carries the presents down the chimneys.

Saint Nicholas drops anchor in the port of Amsterdam, the capital of Holland. December 6 is a special day for Dutch children because they get presents.

Saint Nicholas rides through the city on his large white horse while happy children welcome him. He visits sick children.

On December 6, children search their houses for their presents and read the short poems that come with them. Everyone exchanges gifts.

SAINT NICHOLAS IN AUSTRIA AND SLOVAKIA

In Austria, Saint Nicholas parades through the towns with the *krampus*—strange creatures who threaten to carry disobedient children to hell.

In Slovakia, Saint Nicholas banishes Death from the houses while masked characters watch over him. Death is represented by a ghost carrying a scythe.

SAINT NICHOLAS IN KÜSSNACHT AM RIGI, SWITZERLAND

On the night of December 5, hundreds of people in costumes parade in the streets. People behind Saint Nicholas crack whips above the spectators' heads to chase away evil spirits.

The parade ends with deafening noise. Men dressed in white ring enormous bells. People celebrate all night long.

THE CHRIST CHILD

In certain parts of Germany, France, Switzerland and Austria, the Christ child brings presents.

The Christ child is played by a ten-year-old (often a young girl wearing a white dress and a veil held in place by a crown). Behind the child stands Hans Trapp with a basket full of toys on his back. He also carries a bunch of switches to punish disobedient children with. The Christ child, called "Christkindel," is being replaced by Father Christmas who is getting more and more popular.

45

SWEDISH SANTA CLAUS

Jul Tomte (which means "little Christmas man") is the Swedish Santa Claus. He looks like a dwarf with a white beard.

Originally, Jul Tomte was part of farmers' legends. He didn't have much to do with Christmas and gifts except that, on Christmas Eve, farmers left him food on their doorsteps so he would protect their farms. He became the symbol of Christmas in Sweden when an artist drew him as he is in the picture on the left.

SANTA CLAUS

Santa Claus is known by different names all around the world: Father Christmas in England, *Babbo Natale* in Italy, *Sinter Klass* in Holland and *Weihnachtsmann* in Germany.

Santa Claus was originally Saint Nicholas. When the Dutch immigrated to the United States, *Sinter Klass* (the Dutch name for Saint Nicholas) became Santa Claus. Over time, he became more and more American. He started to look like a jolly round fellow dressed in red with a long white beard. He started to fly though the sky in a sled pulled by reindeer. And that is how we know him today.

SAINT MARTIN'S DAY

Saint Martin is one of the most famous saints in France. He was a very good man who helped the poor and the unhappy. Saint Martin's day (November 11) is the first day of the Christmas season in France.

Saint Martin' day is still celebrated in northern France and some parts of Germany, Belgium and Holland. In France, legend says that one night Saint Martin lost his donkey in the sand dunes and children carrying lanterns found it for him. To thank them, Saint Martin turned his donkey's droppings into cakes. School children in northern France make pretty lanterns out of raw beets every year. They go into the dunes before joining Saint Martin and his donkey for a parade through the town. Saint Martin gives them small cakes.

HALLOWEEN

Before Christmas comes there are many other holidays—such as Halloween. These holidays mark the beginning of the Christmas season that ends in January.

Halloween is celebrated in the United States, Canada and the British Isles. Children go trick-or-treating and grinning jack-o'-lanterns appear everywhere.

JACK-O'-LANTERNS

Where does the tradition of making lanterns out of pumpkins come from? The Irish legend below tells the story of the first jack-o'-lantern.

One night, Jack, a heavy drinker, met the devil in a bar. The devil wanted to take him to hell but Jack suggested he have a drink. The devil changed himself into a coin to pay for his drink. Jack snatched up the coin and popped it into his wallet.

Jack let the devil go but first made him promise not to take him to hell. The devil promised. When Jack died he couldn't get into heaven (because of his sins) or hell (because the devil insisted on keeping his promise).

Jack was upset and asked the devil for a bit of coal to help him find his way in the dark. He put the glowing coal in a turnip and made a lantern. He has been wandering through the dark ever since.

SAINT LUCY

Saint Lucy's day is December 13. In Sweden, people elect
a "Saint Lucy queen" at school, at home and even at work that day.
The winners parade through the streets singing in the evening.

Saint Lucy lived a very long time ago. Legend says that a young man fell in love with her because of her beautiful eyes but went crazy with anger when she wouldn't marry him. He had her arrested and had her eyes poked out. God restored her eyes and, ever since, Saint Lucy is the patron saint of blindness.

In Sweden, Saint Lucy's day (the shortest and darkest day of the year) is celebrated all across the country.

SAINT LUCY'S DAY TODAY

In Sweden, father stays in bed while mother gets the children dressed in long white robes and makes a crown for her daughter to wear on Saint Lucy's day.

Mother and the children load a tray with coffee and lots of muffins and cookies.

The crown of candles is gently placed on the young girl's head.

The whole family wakes up father by singing Saint Lucy's song.

Everyone piles onto the bed to eat breakfast together.

GUY FAWKES DAY

Guy Fawkes day is November 5 and celebrated only in England. Many children take part in the celebrations. There are fireworks displays.

300 years ago, Guy Fawkes and his friends (who all hated the king) wanted to set the parliament building on fire while the king was inside. The king was warned in time and sent his guards. Guy Fawkes was arrested. Every year children go from door to door carrying a straw Guy Fawkes dummy and asking for money to celebrate the event. Later in the night the dummy is burnt on a huge bonfire and fireworks light up the sky.

THE MAGI

The Magi were rich and wise kings. They knew that a savior would one day come and that a marvelous star would announce his birth.

The Magi followed the star to Bethlehem and knelt before the baby Jesus. They brought him expensive gifts: gold (the most valuable metal), frankincense (a kind of incense burnt to honor God), and myrrh (a sweet-smelling ointment used to embalm the dead).

EPIPHANY

"Epiphany" means that God, through Jesus, was revealed to mankind. This Catholic holiday is celebrated on January 6. It is also called "the day of kings" after the Magi.

In France, people eat a special pie with a small figurine hidden inside it to celebrate the day of kings. Whoever finds the figurine is the king and has to choose his queen—or vice versa.

The day of kings is also a popular holiday in Spain (see page 103). In Hungary, children disguised as the Magi carry a creche from door to door asking for money.

THE FIRST TOYS

Ever so long ago, when men still wore animal skins, there was only one kind of toy—rattles carved out of bone or wood.

The first toys were wooden hoops and clay dolls.

Hobby horses were favorite toys for a very long time.

Lead soldiers are another old toy. Young princes were given whole armies of lead soldiers.

Teddy bears were invented at the same time in America and Germany almost 100 years ago.

CHRISTMAS—A TIME OF PEACE AND JOY

These pictures show some of the most important things at Christmas time.

Christmas is thinking of people who are alone.

Christmas is anticipating the big day.

Christmas is getting ready for happiness.

Christmas is getting presents.

Christmas is giving presents.

Christmas is baking cakes and cookies.

Christmas is also the creche and retelling the story of the birth of Jesus, the Son of God.

Christmas is forgiving and making
up after quarrels.

Christmas is decorating
your house and town.

Christmas is laughing, singing
and celebrating.

Christmas is seeing your whole
family and all your friends.

Christmas is lighting up your house.

Christmas is thinking about the baby
Jesus, Joseph and Mary.

THE LITTLE MATCH GIRL

This story was written by Hans Christian Andersen. He was born in 1805 and wrote many other beautiful stories as well.

It was terribly cold on the last evening of the year. A poor little girl, with bare head and naked feet, roamed through the streets.
Her mother had given her slippers but they were too big and the poor little girl had lost them in crossing the street.

A boy had grabbed one up and ran away with it, saying that he could use it as a cradle for his sister's doll.

In an old apron she carried matches to sell.
No one had bought anything from her
the whole day, nor had any one given her even
a penny. Shivering with cold and hunger,
she crept along and sat down in the snow
against a wall.
She dared not go home, for she had sold
no matches, and could not take home
even a penny. Her father would
certainly beat her.

Her little hands were almost frozen with cold. Ah! A burning match might do some good. She drew one out and struck it against the wall.

It gave off a warm, bright light and it seemed to the little girl that she was sitting by a large iron stove. She could finally warm her hands and feet. Alas! She didn't have time—the match burnt out and the stove disappeared.

She rubbed another match on the wall. It burst into flame and she could see into a room on the other side of the wall. A steaming roast goose sat on a beautifully laid table. Suddenly, the goose jumped down from the dish and waddled towards her. Then the match went out, and there remained nothing but the thick, damp, cold wall before her.

She lit another match, and found herself sitting under a beautiful Christmas tree. Thousands of tapers were burning upon the green branches, and colored pictures looked down upon it all.
When the little one stretched out her hands towards them the match went out.

The Christmas lights rose higher and higher, till they looked to her like the stars in the sky. Then she saw a star fall, leaving behind it a bright streak of fire. The little girl thought of her old grandmother, the only one who had ever loved her, and who was now dead.

She rubbed another match on the wall, and a bight light shone round her; she saw her kind, loving grandmother. "Grandmother," cried the little one, "take me with you; I know you will go away when the match burns out; you will vanish like the warm stove, the roast goose and the Christmas tree." And she made haste to light the whole bundle of matches for she wished to keep her grandmother there.

Her grandmother had never appeared so beautiful. She took the little girl in her arms, and they both flew upwards in brightness and joy far above the earth, where there was neither cold nor hunger nor pain, for they were with God.

63

A CHRISTMAS QUIZ

You have met many Christmas characters and will meet many more in this book. Try to answer the questions below. Do your parents and friends know all the answers too?

Which saint leaves presents in good little children's boots on December 6?

What is the name of the saint who is popular in Sweden and whose feast day is December 13?

What is the name of the kind but very ugly witch who brings toys to Italian children?

What is the name of the jolly, white-bearded fellow who leaves presents under the Christmas tree?

CHRISTMAS
CRAFTS

GRAHAM CRACKER YULE LOG

This recipe is easy and quick. It makes a French "bûche"
cake for four people.

a box of
graham
crackers

1 cup
granulated
sugar

1 1/4 cup soft butter

1 cup hot
coffee

7 ounces dark
chocolate

Wrap the graham crackers
in a clean towel and crush
them with a rolling pin.

Put the crumbs in
a mixing bowl.

Add the sugar and butter
and mix well with your hands.

Pour in the hot coffee
and mix well.

Put the dough on a
sheet of aluminum foil.

Roll it into the shape
of a yule log.

Put yule log in the
refrigerator to set.

Cover your "bûche"
with melted chocolate.

CHESTNUT "BÛCHE" CAKE

You need: a 2 lb can of chestnuts, 10 tbsp butter, 2/3 cup granulated sugar, 5 ounces dark chocolate, a mixer, a mixing bowl, a wooden spoon, a pot, a loaf pan, a clean towel, a heavy glass bottle.

for four people

Use a mixer to crush the chestnuts.

Have an adult help you rinse the chestnuts and crush them into paste.

Add the sugar. In a pot, melt 8 tbsp butter and 1 ounce of chocolate over low heat. Add the chocolate mixture to the chestnut paste and mix well.

Put the towel in the loaf pan. Pour in the dough and cover it with the edges of the towel.

Put the bottle on top and put the whole thing in the refrigerator for two days. Take out the "bûche" and place it on a platter. Melt the remaining butter and chocolate together in a pot.

Pour the melted chocolate evenly over the "bûche." Let it cool. Decorate your cake with holly leaves.

A PAPER ANGEL

You can make your own angel for the top of the Christmas tree. You need a large sheet of white paper, a compass, tape and a craft knife.

1-Using the white paper, have an adult help you draw and cut out two squares and a circle.

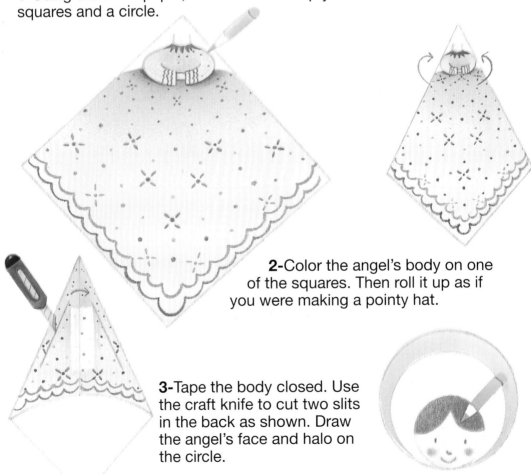

2-Color the angel's body on one of the squares. Then roll it up as if you were making a pointy hat.

3-Tape the body closed. Use the craft knife to cut two slits in the back as shown. Draw the angel's face and halo on the circle.

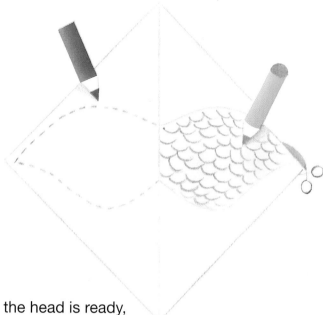

4-When the head is ready, tape it to the body.

5-Draw and color in the angel's wings on the second square. Cut them out.

6-Slide the wings through both slits in the angel's back as shown.

Your angel is all set!

A CHRISTMAS LANTERN

You'll need: 8 1/2 x 11 in. sheets of white paper, felt tip pens, tape, scissors, a pencil and a ruler.

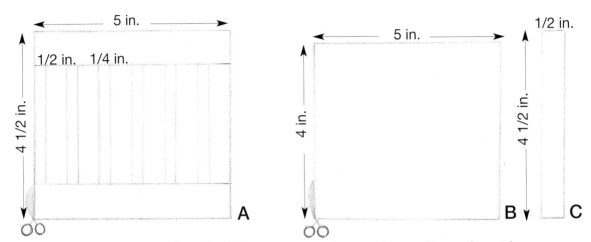

1-Cut out three rectangles of white paper as shown above. Draw the stripes on rectangle A as shown.

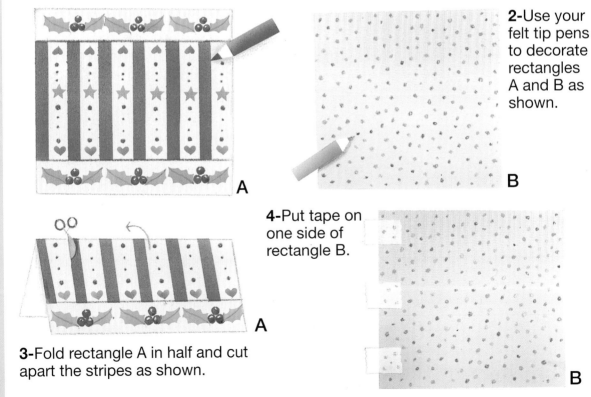

2-Use your felt tip pens to decorate rectangles A and B as shown.

4-Put tape on one side of rectangle B.

3-Fold rectangle A in half and cut apart the stripes as shown.

70

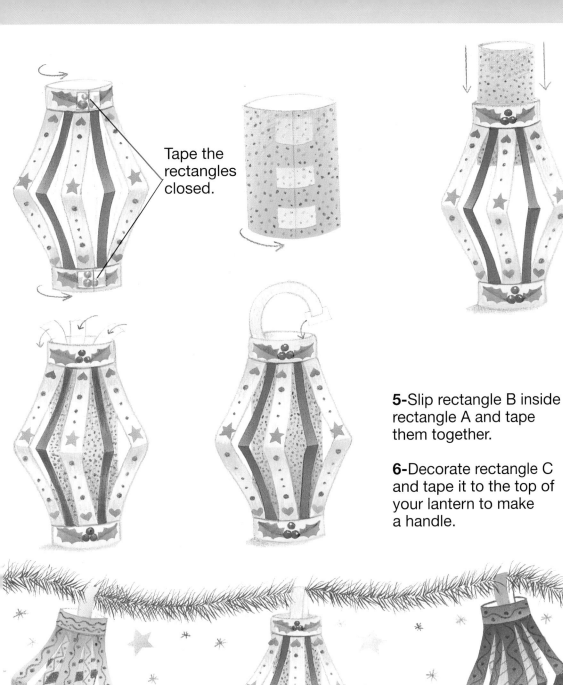

Tape the rectangles closed.

5-Slip rectangle B inside rectangle A and tape them together.

6-Decorate rectangle C and tape it to the top of your lantern to make a handle.

71

CREPE PAPER GARLANDS

These easy-to-make garlands will add color to your house and Christmas tree. You need different colors of crepe paper, glue and scissors.

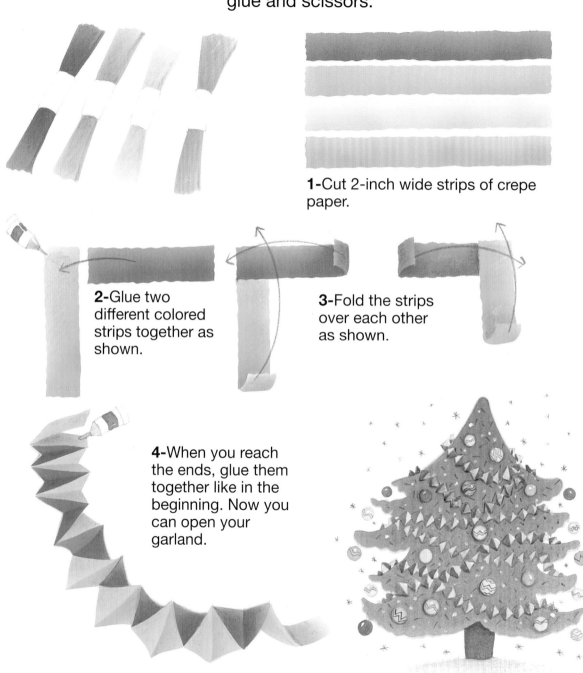

1-Cut 2-inch wide strips of crepe paper.

2-Glue two different colored strips together as shown.

3-Fold the strips over each other as shown.

4-When you reach the ends, glue them together like in the beginning. Now you can open your garland.

RIBBON CHAINS

These ribbon chains are easy to make. You an use them to decorate your Christmas tree, house or dinner table.

Cut off different lengths of brightly colored ribbon.

Make a ring out of a piece of ribbon and tape the ends together. Slip another piece of ribbon through the first ring and tape the second ring closed. Keep adding rings until your ribbon chain is the right length.

A HOST OF ANGELS

You need white paper, a ruler, a pencil, felt tip pens, scissors and tape.

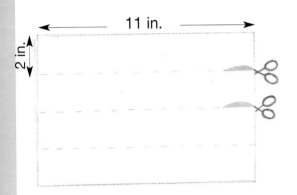

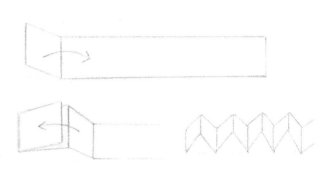

1-Draw and then cut out 2x11 inch strips of paper.

2-Fold the paper strips into accordions as shown.

3-Draw an angel and cut it out through all the layers of paper. Be careful not to cut off the folded edges.

4-Unfold your angel chain and color in all the angels as shown.

5-You can make long angel chains by taping your chains end to end. Now you have a host of angels to decorate your house and Christmas tree!

POMPOM GARLANDS

This garland takes a lot of time to make but it isn't very hard. You'll need different colored yarns, scissors, ribbon and a piece of cardboard.

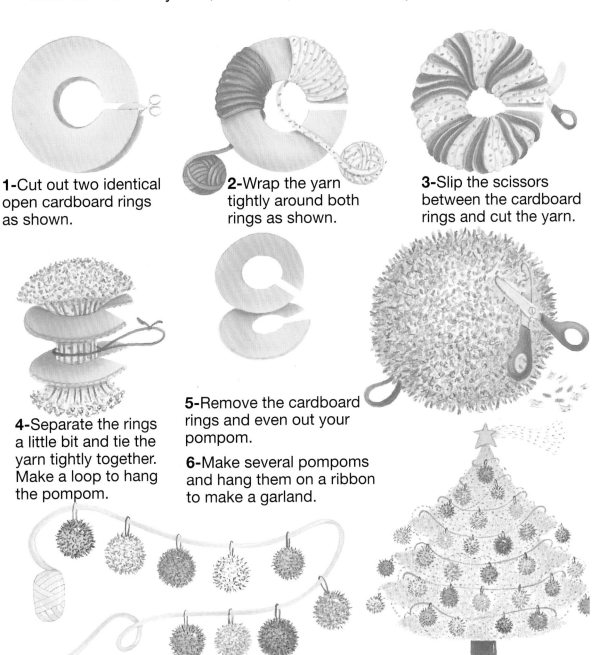

1-Cut out two identical open cardboard rings as shown.

2-Wrap the yarn tightly around both rings as shown.

3-Slip the scissors between the cardboard rings and cut the yarn.

4-Separate the rings a little bit and tie the yarn tightly together. Make a loop to hang the pompom.

5-Remove the cardboard rings and even out your pompom.

6-Make several pompoms and hang them on a ribbon to make a garland.

CHRISTMAS CANDY GARLANDS

Follow the instructions carefully—the hardest part is waiting until after Christmas to eat the candy!

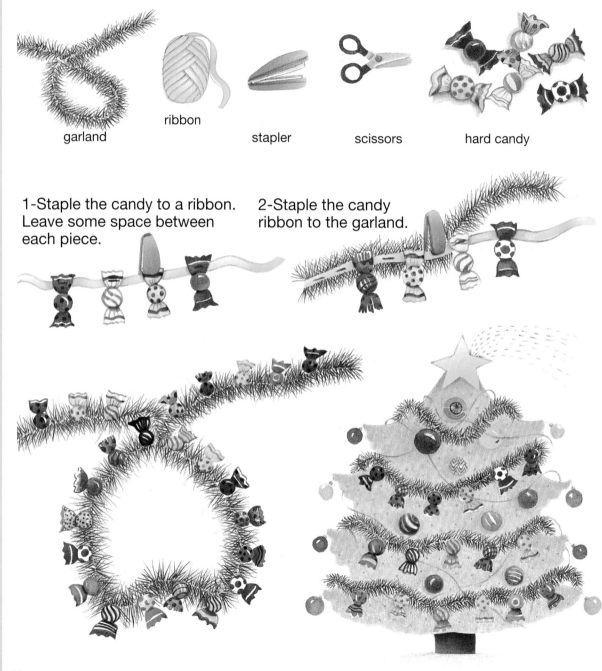

garland

ribbon

stapler

scissors

hard candy

1-Staple the candy to a ribbon. Leave some space between each piece.

2-Staple the candy ribbon to the garland.

A CHRISTMAS PINE CONE

You need pretty pine cones, your favorite color paint and ribbon to make these original decorations.

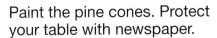

Paint the pine cones. Protect your table with newspaper.

When the pine cones are dry, tie a ribbon around each one and make a pretty bow.

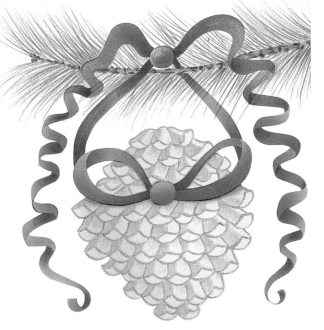

Hang your pine cones on the Christmas tree.

A CHRISTMAS STAR

You need white paper, scissors, tape, a stapler,
aluminum foil and ribbons.

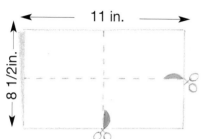

11 in.

8 1/2 in.

1-Cut a piece of paper
into 4 identical rectangles.

2-Cut out a 5th rectangle
the same size as the others.

3-Roll the rectangles
into pointy cones.

4-Tape them all closed.

5-Cover each cone
with aluminum foil.

6-Tape the foil in place.

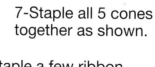

7-Staple all 5 cones
together as shown.

8-Staple a few ribbon
streamers to the
bottom as shown.
Your star is ready
for the tree!

SANDPAPER GINGERBREAD MEN

You can decorate your tree with gingerbread boys and girls made out of sandpaper. You'll need brown sandpaper, a pencil, scissors, a liquid paper pen and ribbon.

the smooth side of the sand paper

1-Draw the outlines of gingerbread boys and girls on the back of the sand paper. Cut them out. (You might want some help from an adult.)

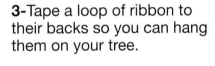

2-Use the liquid paper pen to draw their faces and clothes on the rough side of the sand paper.

3-Tape a loop of ribbon to their backs so you can hang them on your tree.

NAPKIN RINGS

You can made a special napkin ring for each of your guests. You'll need white or gold construction paper, glue, felt tip pens, scissors, a craft knife, a pencil and a ruler.

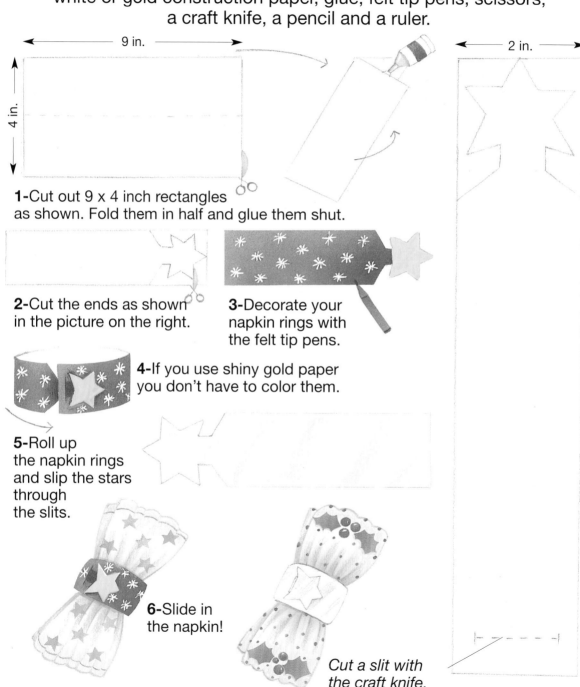

← 9 in. →

4 in.

← 2 in. →

1-Cut out 9 x 4 inch rectangles as shown. Fold them in half and glue them shut.

2-Cut the ends as shown in the picture on the right.

3-Decorate your napkin rings with the felt tip pens.

4-If you use shiny gold paper you don't have to color them.

5-Roll up the napkin rings and slip the stars through the slits.

6-Slide in the napkin!

Cut a slit with the craft knife.

CHRISTMAS PLACE CARDS

You need white paper, pens, glue, scissors, a pencil and a ruler.

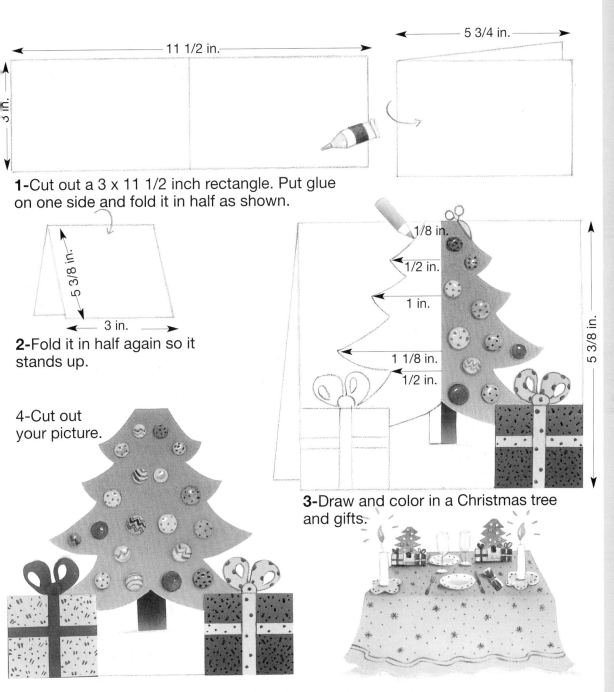

11 1/2 in.

5 3/4 in.

3 in.

1-Cut out a 3 x 11 1/2 inch rectangle. Put glue on one side and fold it in half as shown.

5 3/8 in.

3 in.

2-Fold it in half again so it stands up.

4-Cut out your picture.

1/8 in.

1/2 in.

1 in.

1 1/8 in.

1/2 in.

5 3/8 in.

3-Draw and color in a Christmas tree and gifts.

5-Add your guests' names and put the place cards on the table.

CHRISTMAS DOILIES

You can make your own doilies to put on the dinner table under glasses or bread rolls. You'll need white paper, scissors, glue, aluminum foil and a compass.

1-Cut out a circle or square the size of the doily you want to make and glue aluminum foil to it.

2-Fold your circle or square three times as shown above.

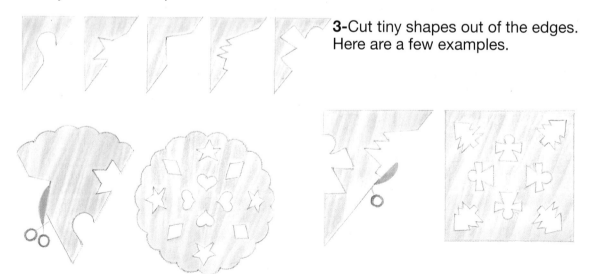

3-Cut tiny shapes out of the edges. Here are a few examples.

4-Unfold your doily. It's as easy as that! Put them silver-side up on the table.

82

STAMP YOUR OWN CHRISTMAS CARDS

You can make your own Christmas card stamps out of potatoes, a knife, paint, a paintbrush and matching paper and envelopes.
Have an adult help you with steps 1 and 2!

1-Cut a potato in half.

2-Use the knife to cut away the potato to make Christmas-shaped stamps as shown.

3-Spread paint on a piece of scrap paper and dip the potato stamps in the paint. Decorate your own Christmas cards and envelopes with the stamps.

SANTA CLAUS STATUE

You need a large egg, a piece of white paper, a fluffy cotton square, tape, glue, a pencil and felt tip pens.

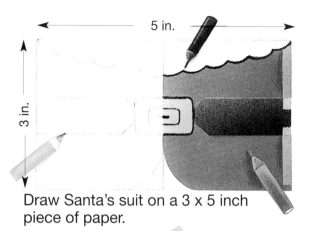

Draw Santa's suit on a 3 x 5 inch piece of paper.

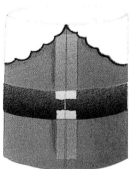

Tape the edges of the rectangle together to make Santa's body.

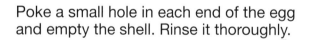

Poke a small hole in each end of the egg and empty the shell. Rinse it thoroughly.

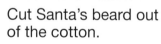

Cut Santa's beard out of the cotton.

Glue the beard to the egg and draw Santa's eyes and nose with a felt tip pen.

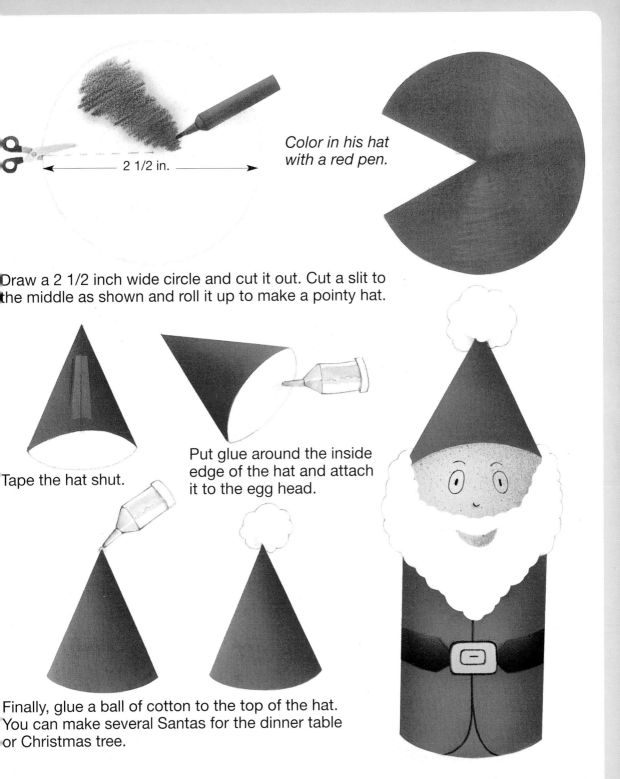

Color in his hat with a red pen.

2 1/2 in.

Draw a 2 1/2 inch wide circle and cut it out. Cut a slit to the middle as shown and roll it up to make a pointy hat.

Tape the hat shut.

Put glue around the inside edge of the hat and attach it to the egg head.

Finally, glue a ball of cotton to the top of the hat. You can make several Santas for the dinner table or Christmas tree.

HOW TO MAKE A JACK-O'-LANTERN FOR HALLOWEEN

Jack-o'-lanterns on doorsteps and on windowsills are part of Halloween (October 31).

You'll need an adult to help you make a jack-o'-lantern. Cut off the top of a pumpkin.

Empty the pumpkin with a large spoon. Scrape the inside well.

Use a sharp knife to cut out the eyebrows, eyes and nose.

Next, cut out a scary mouth with pointy teeth.

Put a candle inside the pumpkin and there you go—a scary head that will make your friends shiver in fright.

AN ADVENT CALENDAR

You'll need: white paper, a pencil, colored pens, glue, tape, scissors, a 15 x 20 in. piece of white cardboard, ribbon and 24 small match boxes.

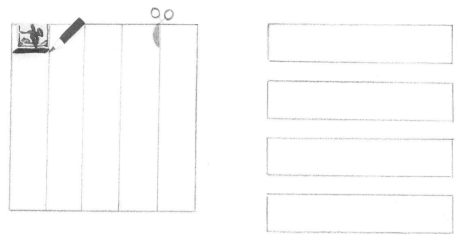

1-Trace lines on a piece of paper as far apart as a match box is wide. Cut the paper into strips along the lines.

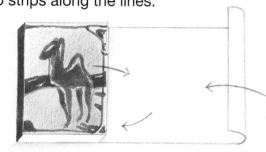

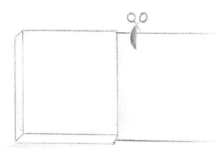

2-Wrap a strip of paper around a match box and cut off the extra paper.

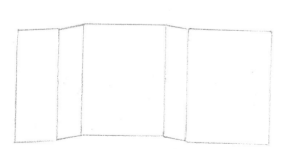

3-You should now have a piece of paper the size and shape of a match box. Flatten the paper and decorate it with a number from 1 to 24 as shown.

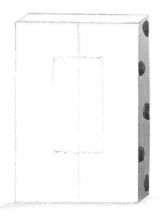

4-When the paper is colored in, wrap it back around the match box and tape it in place. Do the same thing to the 23 remaining boxes. Give each one a different number between 1 and 24.

5-Glue your 24 decorated match boxes to the white cardboard in random order.

6-Color in the edges of your calendar and decorate it with ribbons. Attach a long ribbon to the top so that you can hang it on the wall.

When your Advent calendar is ready, give it to your parents so they can put a surprise in each and every box. This way, you'll have a present a day until Christmas. Open the first box on December 1.

MORE CHRISTMAS TREE DECORATIONS

These small decorations are very easy to make and add color to your Christmas tree.

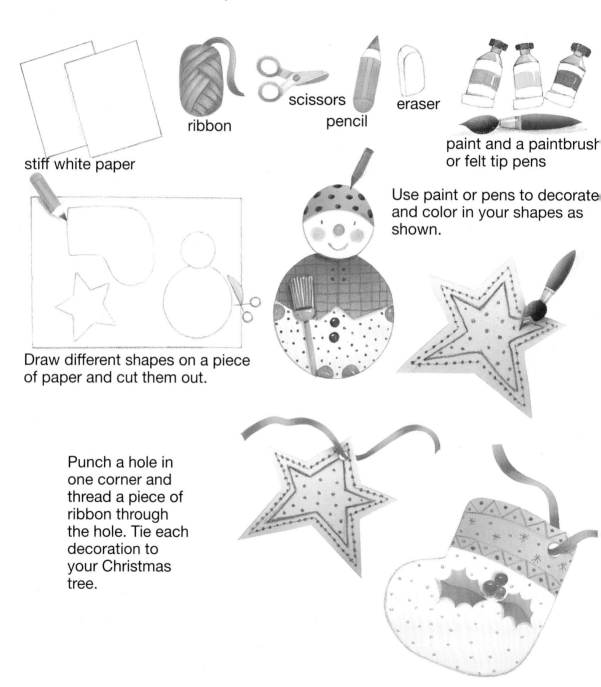

ribbon

scissors

pencil

eraser

paint and a paintbrush or felt tip pens

stiff white paper

Use paint or pens to decorate and color in your shapes as shown.

Draw different shapes on a piece of paper and cut them out.

Punch a hole in one corner and thread a piece of ribbon through the hole. Tie each decoration to your Christmas tree.

CHRISTMAS AROUND THE WORLD

CHRISTMAS IN GERMANY

As in many other countries, German children start getting ready for Christmas in the beginning of December.

Some families make their own Advent calendars with garlands and tiny presents.

A candle on the wreath is lit every Sunday during Advent.

Forsythia branches are put in vases of water on Saint Barbara's day (December 4). They flower at Christmas.

There are lots of special Christmas cookies to be made. Children help their mothers.

On December 24, during the night, either the Christ child or Father Christmas brings presents and puts them under the tree.

Children all put their boots outside their bedroom doors on Saint Nicholas's day.

Everyone helps decorate the Christmas tree on December 24. What a festive sight! What a lot of fun!

Yummy! A roasted goose with red cabbage and potatoes for Christmas Eve dinner.

On the day of kings, children dress up as the Magi and write the initials of the three wise men on people's front doors.

CHRISTMAS IN ENGLAND

People send Christmas cards to their friends and family early in December. They decorate the walls with the cards they get. They are taken down on January 6, the day of kings.

Some of the cards are glued to ribbons and hung on the walls.

The whole house is decked in green and red.

The whole family has fun decorating the Christmas tree.

Many children write letters to Father Christmas.

While Father Christmas is hitching up his reindeer and loading his sled with toys, children wait impatiently for him to come.
The whole family gets ready for the big day.

Children go caroling on Christmas Eve. People give them little presents and candy in exchange for the songs.

Children hang stockings at the foot of their beds.

Cookies and a glass of port are left out for Father Christmas.

Children fall asleep thinking of Father Christmas on Christmas Eve. Is he going to bring all the toys they asked for?

Christmas wouldn't be Christmas without turkey with chestnut stuffing and Christmas pudding.

Bang! When you pull open a Christmas cracker it makes a popping noise.

CHRISTMAS IN AUSTRIA

Christmas is the most important family holiday of the year. Movie theaters, restaurants and theaters all close their doors on Christmas Eve. Everyone gets to celebrate.

Christmas starts with the Advent wreath on December 1.

There are Christmas trees in every town and city square.

The streets are full of children and their grandparents on December 24. Their parents are busy decorating the Christmas tree that has been hidden in the attic or basement until then.

The whole month of December is a party around the city hall in Vienna, the capital. The trees in the park are covered in wonderful, fairy-tale decorations!

The "baby Jesus market" takes place in this same magical park. It is a Christmas fair where wide-eyed children warm their hands on paper cones filled with roast chestnuts.

Future figure skating stars disguised as animals or fairy tale creatures spin on the ice skating rink in the park. It is a charming show that children love to see.

Children can ride a small train across the park. Before the whistle blows, they can write down what they want for Christmas on a blackboard that Father Christmas and baby Jesus are said to read.

CHRISTMAS IN DENMARK

Christmas celebrations last the whole month of December. Streets are lit up and decorated with garlands and pine branches.

Children send lots of Christmas cards to their friends and family. Special postage stamps are sold for Christmas. One of the prettiest ones was drawn by the queen herself.

A wreath with four candles is hung from the ceiling.

The whole family goes into the forest to cut down their Christmas tree.

CHRISTMAS IN DENMARK

Houses are decorated with pine branches, tiny angels, elves and straw stars as soon as the Christmas season starts.

Children make most of their own decorations for the Christmas tree.

Christmas dinner traditionally starts at six o'clock. At the end of the meal rice pudding with a whole almond hidden in it is served. Whoever finds the almond gets a good-luck marzipan pig.

After dinner, father goes into the room where the Christmas tree is and decorates it by himself with garlands of Danish flags, candles and small red and white hearts.

He lights the candles one by one while the rest of the family waits impatiently in the next room.

When the tree is ready the family comes in and forms a circle around the tree. Everyone takes turns choosing Christmas carols and they sing and dance around the tree.

CHRISTMAS IN SPAIN

Spanish children are lucky. They get presents on December 25 and on January 6 when the Magi leave gifts in their slippers.

Many large cities have Magi processions. They are very popular—the Magi parade by on richly decorated floats, followed by men on horseback. Children and adults crowd on the sidewalks to see them go by.

After the parade the Magi join the crowd. Children are very impressed when they get to meet the Magi close-up

CHRISTMAS IN FINLAND

Finnish children are very busy on Christmas Eve. In the morning they set off in sleds to cut down their Christmas trees and they spend the afternoon decorating them.

Santa Claus is supposed to come from Lapland (an area north of Norway, Sweden and Finland). Santa Claus gets more than 500,000 letters every year at the North Pole.

On December 24, people light candles on graves.

The Christmas tree is taken down twenty days after Christmas.

CHRISTMAS IN FRANCE

The cities and towns in France take on a holiday air several weeks before Christmas (like many other countries around the world).

City halls all across the country are decorated with garlands of lights. People set up huge Christmas trees in town squares.

The trees along main streets are covered with lights. The long winter nights are jollier thanks to millions of tiny lights.

Department stores decorate their windows. Some put on animated shows. People crowd the sidewalks to stare at the wonderful displays.

Children have their pictures taken with Father Christmas.

Primary school children decorate their classrooms.

CHRISTMAS IN THE PROVENCE REGION

Provence is a region in the south of France. The Christmas traditions there are different from in the rest of the country.

In some churches near the seaside Midnight Mass ends with a procession of fishermen who lay a basket full of fish at the foot of the altar as a sign of friendship and gratitude towards the baby Jesus.

Christmas Eve dinner traditionally ends with thirteen desserts that are supposed to symbolize Christ and the twelve apostles. These desserts are made out of all the fruits and sweets of the region.

CHRISTMAS IN IRELAND

Christmas celebrations start twelve days before Christmas.
This period of time is called Little Christmas.

A candle is put on the windowsill on Christmas day. A glass of whisky for Father Christmas and carrots for his reindeer are set out before the family goes to Midnight Mass.

Presents are opened on Christmas morning.

Christmas dinner is served at 2 or 3 o'clock in the afternoon.

The day after Christmas, December 26, is Stephen's Day. Many Irish people go to see horse races while others sing in the streets.

The day after Christmas is another day of celebration. In Irish cities people get together to bet on horses.

Young boys—the Wren Boys—dress in old-fashioned clothes and sing and play music in the countrysides. They go from house to house to ask for a few coins.

CHRISTMAS IN ICELAND

As in all Christian countries, Christmas is the children's holiday.
The Christmas season ends with singing and dancing around
bonfires on the day of kings, January 6.

Jol means Christmas in Icelandic. The *Jolasveinar* are small Christmas elves. You
can read more about them on the next page.

Children put their shoes on the windowsill at the beginning of December. If they are
good they get a small present from Father Christmas but if they are bad they get a
potato!

JOLASVEINAR

There are thirteen of these elves. Their names say a lot about their personalities. They are Gryla's children. Gryla is a monstrous three-headed creature.

Gryla has three bearded goat heads. His favorite food is the flesh of bad children who can only escape him by becoming good. His children have funny names: Pot-licker, Sausage-stealer, Window-watcher, etc. They used to pester people and their pets, steal animals, slam doors and so on. When Father Christmas made his appearance, the legend changed. The elves got nicer and now they spend their time making presents for good boys and girls.

CHRISTMAS IN ITALY

Christmas traditions are different from one region to the next and Italian children don't all get presents on the same day.

In some parts of northern Italy, either *Babbo Natale* (Father Christmas) or *Gesù Bambino* (baby Jesus) brings presents on December 25. Elsewhere, Saint Lucy brings toys on December 13.

In Rome, the capital, Befana brings toys on the day of the kings. Befana is an old witch but she is very nice. She flies on her broomstick and brings packages down the chimneys.

CHRISTMAS IN MOLDAVIA

Christmas celebrations last twelve days in this country in southeastern Europe. There are many parades in towns and cities.

CHRISTMAS IN NORWAY

The whole family starts getting the Christmas tree decorations ready on the first day of December. The first candle on the Advent wreath is lit.

Houses are decorated. The wreath on the front door shows that people are getting ready for Christmas. Straw goats and sheaves of wheat are put in front of the houses

A star is hung in every window.

A candle is placed on every grave on December 24.

Flowers are part of the Christmas decorations in Norway. Tulips and hyacinth are placed all over the house to give it a festive air.

People buy potted tulips so that they last longer.

Mother makes delicious heart-shaped waffles.

Sled rides are a fun part of Christmas. Dress warmly and slip under wolf pelts—and don't forget your lantern because night falls early in the afternoon.

Before opening their presents the whole family sings and dances around the Christmas tree after dinner. This very old custom is still one of children's favorite parts of Christmas.

The family forms two circles—one big and one small—around the Christmas tree. Once everyone is singing the first circle turns to the right and the second to the left. When the song is over, everyone changes circles and they start over with another song.

CHRISTMAS IN POLAND

On Christmas Eve, children watch the skies for the first star because it marks the beginning of dinner and the celebrations.

People slip straw under the tablecloth when they set the table to remind themselves that Jesus was born in a stable. An empty place is always set in case a surprise guest shows up.

After dinner, the family says a prayer and shares a kind of rectangular host cracker called *oplateck*. On it is a bas-relief image of Joseph and Mary or the Christ child. Everyone makes a wish and quarrels are forgotten.

CHRISTMAS IN POLAND

The Christmas season traditionally starts on December 24 and ends on January 6, the day of kings.

Groups of children disguised as the Magi, devils, angels and shepherds go from door to door on Christmas Eve asking for money and cookies.

Sometimes people go on sled rides in the snow-covered countryside and have picnics on Christmas. They light fires and grill sausages.

CHRISTMAS IN SLOVAKIA

The most important day of Advent is December 6. Children shine their shoes and put them on the windowsill so Saint Nicholas can put small presents in them.

Many families with small children give parties for Saint Nicholas. Adults dress up as Saint Nicholas, the devil and angels. Children sing and get presents.

The "twelve holy days" fall between Christmas and Epiphany. During this period, ceremonies and gatherings of people keep alive popular traditions celebrating the end of winter.

CHRISTMAS IN SWITZERLAND

Christmas for Swiss children is mostly about having fun sledding, skiing and playing in the snow.

Chalets and Christmas trees are decorated with strings of lights. Children get packages containing an orange, a bar of chocolate and a sugar roll before getting their presents from Father Christmas.

CHRISTMAS IN SWEDEN

The Christmas month is very busy! Everyone works hard evenings and weekends getting ready for the big day.

Every Sunday a candle on the yule log is lit.

Children discover a present hidden in the calendar every day.

A sheaf of wheat is placed in the garden for the birds.

There are lots of Christmas cookies to be made.

CHRISTMAS IN SWEDEN

Houses are decorated right before Christmas. The best Christmas flowers are red but there are also pink, white and pale blue ones.

The Christmas tree is decorated with straw figures.

A good-luck charm is placed at the foot of the tree.

The smell of hyacinths fills the air at Christmas.

The traditional Christmas dish is a whole ham, either roast or boiled.

Christmas presents are called *joklappar* which means "Christmas knocks" because a long time ago people knocked very loudly on the door of the person they wanted to give a present to. When the door opened, they would throw the present inside and run away before they could be recognized.

After dinner, people wait for Father Christmas. When he arrives he knocks on the door and calls out, "Are there any good children here?"

Each present comes with its own poem. The poems are often funny and people read them out loud. The family dances around the Christmas tree for the last time on January 13.

CHRISTMAS IN QUEBEC, CANADA

"Father Christmas's kingdom" is set up in many shopping centers in November. You can meet Father Christmas there.

There is a Christmas parade every year in Montreal. The parade is organized by a department store. Lots and lots of people come to applaud Father Christmas even though it is very cold out.

Father Christmas comes at the end of the parade. When the parade is over, he flies away on his sled while wide-eyed children stare after him.

Christmas in Quebec is a magical time of year. Snow lays gently over everything, the streets are full and houses and stores are festive sights.

People in Quebec decorate the outsides of their houses with strings of lights, pine branches and ribbons. They put small Christmas trees covered with lights at the edge of the streets.

The Canadian postal service receives thousands of letters for Father Christmas.

Milk and cookies are left near the fireplace for Father Christmas.

CHRISTMAS IN THE UNITED STATES

Christmas is a very popular holiday in the United States. Immigrants from all over the world brought their traditions with them when they came.

The whole family helps decorate the house. Stockings are hung by the chimney, Christmas cards are displayed and popcorn strings are made to decorate the tree.

Candy canes are hung on the branches of the Christmas tree.

Mailboxes are full of Christmas cards from friends and family.

Turkey, a Christmas dish in many countries around the world, was discovered by the first immigrants to the United States.

People decorate the outsides of their houses with strings of electric lights.

People go caroling and are sometimes invited inside for a glass of eggnog.

Santa Claus is a jolly old fellow dressed in red.

Christmas dinner on December 25 is a large roast turkey.

PUMPKIN PIE

Pumpkin pie is a traditional part of Thanksgiving and Christmas. Here's how to make one.

You need: 1 1/2 cups cooked or canned pumpkin, 1 1/2 cups evaporated milk, 1/2 cup milk, 2 beaten eggs, 1 cup sugar, 1/2 tsp salt, 1 1/2 tsp cinnamon, 1/2 tsp powdered ginger, and 1/2 tsp ground cloves. Don't forget a ready-made pie crust.

Peal the pumpkin and cut the flesh into pieces.

Cook them for twenty minutes in salted water.

Mash the cooked pumpkin.

Add all the ingredients and beat until smooth.

Line a pie pan with the pie crust and pour in the pumpkin mixture.

Bake the pie for about 45 minutes in a 300°F preheated oven.

CHRISTMAS IN MEXICO

Christmas celebrations start on December 16. Families in many villages reenact Joseph and Mary's voyage to Bethlehem.

One family goes to the church to get the figurines of Joseph and Mary. They are dressed as travelers and firmly attached to a stretcher.

Two young girls carry the stretcher to a house chosen in advance and ask for hospitality. Joseph and Mary are placed on a waiting altar and decorated with flowers.

The couple travels for eight days. Each evening they go to a different house where there is a party for children with a *piñata*. On December 24, Joseph and Mary are placed near the baby Jesus in the creche in front of the church.

Piñatas are hollow clay animals or other figures filled with candy and small toys. Blindfolded children hit them with sticks to break them open and get the treats inside.

Joseph and Mary are placed in the creche on the ninth day.

Huge luminous decorations cover the walls in large cities.

CHRISTMAS IN AUSTRALIA

Australians celebrate the birth of Jesus in the middle of summer heat. Christmas dinner is often a roast turkey or goose and a Christmas pudding like in England.

Some Australians celebrate Christmas at the beach with a huge picnic of cold turkey, salads and cakes. At home in the evening they gather around a beautifully decorated Christmas tree.

ISBN 2-215-06262-2
Printed in Italy (06-99).